MORDICAI GERSTEIN

Noah
and the
Great Flood

SIMON & SCHUSTER BOOKS FOR YOUNG READERS

SIMON & SCHUSTER BOOKS FOR YOUNG READERS
An imprint of Simon & Schuster Children's Publishing Division
1230 Avenue of the Americas
New York, New York 10020
Copyright © 1999 by Mordicai Gerstein
All rights reserved including the right of reproduction in whole
or in part in any form.
SIMON & SCHUSTER BOOKS FOR YOUNG READERS
is a trademark of Simon & Schuster.
Book design by Lucille Chomowicz
The text of this book is set in Hiroshige.
The artwork was created with oil paint on vellum.
Printed in Hong Kong
First Edition 10 9 8 7 6 5 4 3 2 1
Library of Congress Cataloging-in-Publication Data
Gerstein, Mordicai.
Noah and the great flood / Mordicai Gerstein. p. cm.
Summary: A retelling of the Old Testament story of how
Noah and his family were saved, along with two of
every living creature, when God destroyed the
wicked of the world with a devastating flood.
ISBN 0-689-81371-6
1. Noah (Biblical figure)—Juvenile literature.
2. Noah's ark—Juvenile literature.
Bible stories, English—O.T.—Genesis. [1. Noah (Biblical figure)
2. Noah's ark. 3. Bible stories—O.T.] I. Title. BS580.N6G47 1999
222'.1109505—dc21 97-19259

For my grandfather, William Chornow

According to the Bible there once lived, in the earliest days,

a race of giants, three thousand ells tall.

Their mothers were human but their fathers were angels.

The giants were greedy and violent and they turned away from God.

Only one man pleased God at that time. His name was Noah.

God chose Noah to help him make the world over.

After the great flood, it is told that Noah planted vineyards,

and then divided the lands and languages of the world up

among his three sons, so that all people are descendents of Noah.

In the Jewish tradition, many legends have arisen around

the stories of the Bible.

These legends fill out the stories with details that bring us closer to the action.

They tell us how people and things really looked,

how big and how many of them they were,

and what happened before and after.

Here, then, is the story of Noah, enriched by these legends.

It is told that Noah was born with sunlight streaming from his eyes.
Light of every color filled the house.
"What does this mean?" everyone asked.
"It means," said his great-grandfather, who was three hundred and
sixty-five years old and very wise, "that one day, because of Noah,
there will be a bridge of light between heaven and earth,
and the world will end and begin again."

Noah grew up to be kind and generous. He loved all living things.

He became a farmer and invented the shovel, the hoe, and the plow.

At the age of four hundred and ninety-eight, Noah married Naamah.

They had three sons: Shem, Ham, and Japheth,

who were all as kind and generous as their father.

God looked down and was pleased.

But most of the people of that long-ago time were cruel, selfish giants.

They filled the air with anger and curses and violence.

God looked down on them and was not pleased.

"I regret having created this world." He sighed.

One afternoon Noah heard the voice of God.

"Noah," said the voice, "of all the people on earth,

only you and your family please me.

Go and warn all the others that they must stop being greedy, violent,

and cruel, or I will destroy the world with a great flood."

"I will warn them, Lord," said Noah. "Please don't destroy the world."

Every day, for one hundred and twenty years,
Noah warned the people, pleading, "Please change your ways,
or God will destroy the world with a great flood!"
"Floods can't hurt us," sneered the giants. "We are so tall, our heads
will always be above the water!"

And Noah said to God, "Lord, the people won't listen to me.
What shall I do?"
Clouds gathered. Noah heard distant thunder.
"Noah," said the voice of God, "the time has come to build an ark.
Make it of gopher wood. Build it three hundred cubits long,
fifty cubits wide, and thirty cubits high."

"But Lord," said Noah, "I don't know how to build an ark.

I don't know what an ark is."

And so the angel Raphael brought a book to Noah.

It was made of sapphires, and it glowed with light.

"This book was shown to Adam, the first man," said the angel.

"It contains all the wisdom of the world. It will help you build the ark."

Then Noah, with his wife and sons, began to build the ark, and the ark helped build itself. The wood divided without being cut, and the hammers and nails seemed to know what to do. All the while, the giants jeered and the sky grew darker.

And when the ark was finished God said,
"Noah, gather food and provisions, and a male and female
of every kind of creature that lives on the earth."
"But Lord," said Noah, "how will I gather all those animals?"

Even as he spoke, the animals began to come.

Marching and galloping, flying and crawling, trotting and scurrying,

a male and female of each kind hurried into the ark.

"Noah is starting a zoo!" snickered the giants.

There were animals no one knew existed.

One, who called himself an og, was so big he didn't fit in the ark.

So he and his wife sat snug on the roof.

Another, called a rayeem, was even bigger.

Noah tied her and her husband to ropes

so they might swim behind the ark.

On the day that Noah was six hundred years, two months,
and seventeen days old, and all the animals were on board,
lightning flashed, thunder crashed, and it began to rain.
"Friends!" Noah cried to the giants, for he cared for all living things.
"Change your ways. There is still time!"
But the giants laughed and splashed in the puddles.
Noah and his family entered the ark and God locked the door.

Not only did rain pour from the sky,
but great fountains spurted out of the ground.
The water rose and the ark began to float.
"Noah!" called the now-frightened giants. "Save us!"

"I cannot," wept Noah. "God has locked the door!"

Day after day the water grew higher.

The giants disappeared.

Even the tallest mountain disappeared. And still the rain fell.

Naamah cooked for Noah and her sons. Noah fed the wild animals.

Shem fed the tame ones. Ham took care of the birds.

Japheth tended the reptiles.

Some animals were fed by day. Others were fed by night.

The lion was impatient for his food and struck Noah on the leg.
"That's the way of lions," Noah thought with a shrug,
though he limped ever after.

The urshanas said, "Don't worry about us. Feed the others first."
Noah smiled. "May the Lord let you live forever," he said.
And they live happily to this very day, though no one knows where.

Noah fed the ogs through a hole in the roof.

He fed the rayeems from the back of the ark.
And always, day and night, the rain continued falling.
"I'm afraid it will never stop," thought Noah.

But finally, after forty days and forty nights, the rain stopped.

Noah looked out and saw nothing but water.

He waited three hundred and twenty-five days.

Then he sent the dove out to look for dry land.

The dove flew far but found nowhere to perch and so returned.

A week later, Noah sent her out again.

She flew up to heaven and the angel Gabriel gave her a branch of olive.
"This is a sign from God," said Noah. "The flood is over."

Then the water lowered and disappeared,
and the ark came to rest on the very top of Mount Ararat.
God opened the door and said,
"Noah, everyone may come out of the ark now."
But Noah said, "Forgive me, Lord, but we won't come out unless
you promise that there will never be another flood like this one,
and that you will never destroy the world again."

And God said, "I promise.
I know that you and your family will work hard
to make a more peaceful and beautiful world.
And as a sign, I will make a bridge of light between heaven and earth.
When you, your children, or your children's children see it,
you will all remember my promise, and so will I.
Always."

And so Noah and his family and all the animals
thanked God and left the ark.
And the world began again.